P9-DOD-710

CARL

and the
Meaning
of Life

Deborah Freedman

Viking

Carl was not a **bird**.

RO456309927

Carl was
not a **bear**,

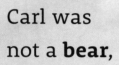

or a **beaver**.

Carl was . . .

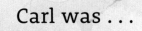

an **earthworm**.

He lived underground, moving, moving, always moving, burrowing, tunneling, digesting dead leaves, feasting and casting, turning hard dirt into fluffy soil, day after day . . .

"Why?"
asked a field mouse gathering seeds.
"Why do you do that?"

Why?

Carl did not know *why*.

But now he needed to find out.

So Carl stopped making fluffy soil.

"I'll be right back!"
he told the field mouse.

He spotted a rabbit.
Maybe she knew.

"Why do I do what I do?"
he asked her.

"Oh, goodness, dear," she said.
"I do not know. *I* do what I do for my babies!"

But Carl did not have babies.

A fox appeared.
Carl turned to the fox.

"Why do I do what I do?" asked Carl.
"Who do I do it for?"

"For *whom*," replied the fox.

"Alas, my meal awaits. I am here for the hunt."

But Carl did not want to hunt.

"Why are you talking to a fox?!"
cried a squirrel.

Carl was startled.
"Because the field mouse is waiting
and wants to know what I am here for!"

The squirrel declared,
"*I'm* here to plant trees.
Trees are where I sleep."

But Carl could not sleep—
not high in a tree,
and not without an answer
for the mouse.

He pushed on . . .

"What?"

. . . and on.
Hours turned into days, until
the soil was no longer fluffy.

The ground around Carl
turned barren and dry . . .

"Who?"

while he continued to search.

"Why?"

sigh...

But the birds had flown off to find grasses and fluff . . .
the bear trundled away to look for berries . . .
soon there was nobody left to talk to.

"What about me?" called Carl.

The clouds were silent.
So was the air.

I will never find out. He sniffled.

Then Carl heard his sniffle echo.
Followed by a squeak. . . .

"I can't find any grubs!" a voice cried.
It was the saddest ground beetle he had ever seen.
Carl peeked under a stone. No grubs.

Then he poked at the dirt.
It was hard, like rock!
Where was his fluffy soil?

Suddenly Carl knew
what he needed to do.
"I'll be back!" he promised.

For hours into days, weeks into months, Carl munched,

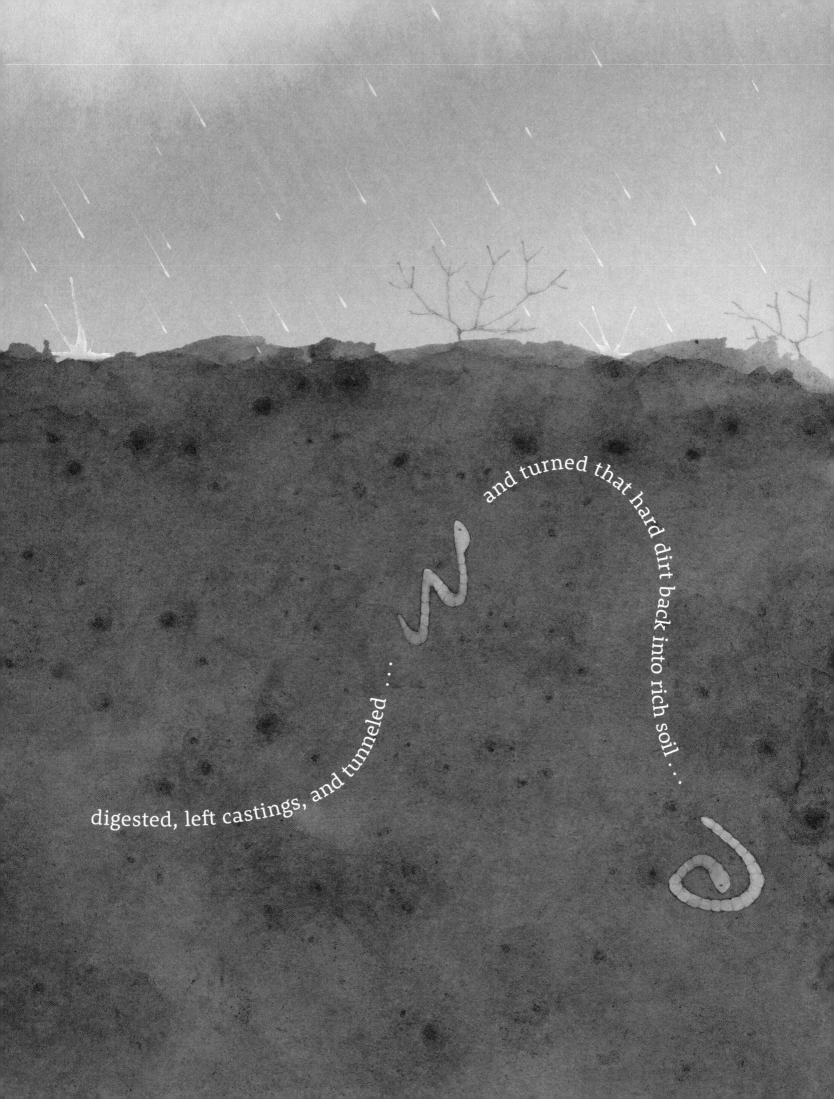

and turned that hard dirt back into rich soil . . .

digested, left castings, and tunneled . . .

"You made my seeds grow!"
said the mouse.

Clover blossomed once again,
and the rabbit came back with her kits.
The squirrel returned to plant new trees,

the fox was lured by the hunt,
all of them able to do what they do . . .

HOW?

Well, why not ask Carl?

Author's Note

HAVE YOU EVER watched squirrels running around or beetles skittering by and wondered, "What are they doing?" or "Why do they do that?"

Just like Carl, every creature in this book has an important job. The mouse, rabbit, squirrel, fox, and ground beetle all need each other, and our world needs them. Everything is connected—including you!

How do **you** help the earth?

_____

"It may be doubted whether there are many other animals which have played so important a part in the history of the world, as have these lowly organized creatures."

—Charles Darwin*

*THE FORMATION OF VEGETABLE MOULD, THROUGH
THE ACTION OF WORMS, with Observations on Their Habits,
by Charles Darwin, 1883

Dedicated to:
Kendra Levin and Stephen Barr—for doing what you do—

with Jim Hoover and Denise Cronin and Ken Wright and everyone at
Viking Children's Books and Penguin Young Readers. Many thanks!

VIKING
Penguin Young Readers
An imprint of Penguin Random House LLC
375 Hudson Street
New York, New York 10014

First published in the United States of America by Viking,
an imprint of Penguin Random House LLC, 2019

Copyright © 2019 by Deborah Freedman

Penguin supports copyright. Copyright fuels creativity, encourages diverse voices, promotes
free speech, and creates a vibrant culture. Thank you for buying an authorized edition of this book
and for complying with copyright laws by not reproducing, scanning, or distributing any part of it
in any form without permission. You are supporting writers and allowing Penguin to continue
to publish books for every reader.

LIBRARY OF CONGRESS CATALOGING-IN-PUBLICATION DATA IS AVAILABLE
ISBN: 9780451474988

Manufactured in China
Book design by Jim Hoover and Deborah Freedman
This book is set in Rooney and Boho

The illustrations were made with pencil, watercolor, and bits of colored pencil,
and assembled in Photoshop.

10   9   8   7   6   5   4   3   2